♡Eva and the New Owl♡

Read more OWL DIARIES books!

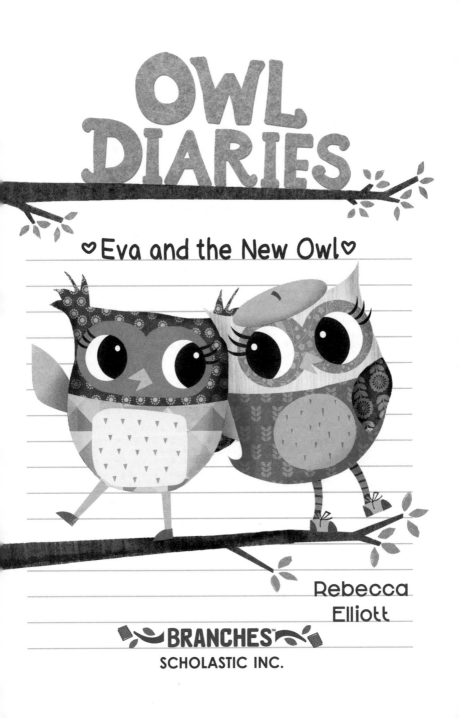

OWL DIARIES

♡Eva and the New Owl♡

Rebecca Elliott

BRANCHES
SCHOLASTIC INC.

For Matthew, my best friend. —R.E.

Special thanks to Eva Montgomery.

The publisher does not have any control over and does not assume
any responsibility for author or third-party websites or their content.

No part of this publication may be reproduced, stored in a retrieval system,
or transmitted in any form or by any means, electronic, mechanical,
photocopying, recording, or otherwise, without written permission of the
publisher. For information regarding permission, write to Scholastic Inc.,
Attention: Permissions Department, 557 Broadway, New York, NY 10012.

This book is a work of fiction. Names, characters, places, and incidents are
either the product of the author's imagination or are used fictitiously, and any
resemblance to actual persons, living or dead, business establishments,
events, or locales is entirely coincidental.

Library of Congress Cataloging-in-Publication Data

Elliott, Rebecca, author.
Eva and the new owl / Rebecca Elliott. — First edition.
pages cm. — (Owl diaries ; 4)
Summary: Eva wants to be friends with Hailey, the new owl in her class,
but when Hailey seems to prefer Lucy's company, Eva starts to feel left out,
and even a little jealous of her best friend.
ISBN 0-545-82559-8 (pbk. : alk. paper) — ISBN 0-545-82560-1 (hardcover : alk. paper)
1. Owls—Juvenile fiction. 2. Best friends—Juvenile fiction. 3. Jealousy—Juvenile fiction.
4. Elementary schools—Juvenile fiction. 5. Diaries—Juvenile fiction. [1. Owls—Fiction. 2.
Best friends—Fiction. 3. Friendship—Fiction. 4. Jealousy—
5. Schools—Fiction. 6. Diaries—Fiction.] I. Title. II. Series:
Elliott, Rebecca. Owl diaries ; 4.
PZ7.E45812Ep 2016
[Fic]—dc23

2015027416
ISBN 978-0-545-82560-3 (hardcover) / ISBN 978-0-545-82559-7 (paperback)

10 9 8 7 6 5 4 3   16 17 18 19 20

Printed in the United States of America.   113
First edition, May 2016

Book design by Marissa Asuncion
Edited by Katie Carella

♡ Table of Contents ♡

1

♥ I'm Back! ♥

Thursday

Hello Diary,
    Look who's back! It's me – Eva
Wingdale! Your feathery friend!

<u>I love</u>:

Writing stories

Stargazing

Picnics

My new slippers

Blueberry ice cream

Playing **WINGBALL**

The word <u>bumblebee</u>

Sleepovers

<u>I DO NOT love</u>:

The word <u>slime</u>

Tying my shoelaces

Spelling tests

Mom's bug salad

Washing dishes

Baby Mo's
stinky diapers

Squirrels stealing
our food (unless it's
Mom's bug salad)

Feeling left out

I REALLY love my family!

Here's our holiday card picture:

Dad

Mom

Humphrey

Baby Mo

Me

the Wingdales

I also love my pet bat, Baxter. He's part of the family, too!

Owls are amazing. I love, love, love being an owl!

We are awake ALL night.

We are asleep ALL day.

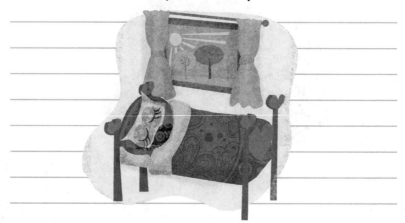

We can fly without making any noise.

And we can hear things a long way away.

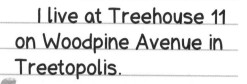

I live at Treehouse 11 on Woodpine Avenue in Treetopolis.

My next-door neighbor is my BEST friend, Lucy Beakman.

9

Lucy has a pet lizard named Rex. Rex and Baxter are best friends. We love dressing up our pets.

Rex →

Lucy and I go to school together. Here is our class photo:

Mrs. Featherbottom
Kiera Zac
Macy Sue
Carlos

my class

Lilly
Zara Me Jacob
George Lucy

Now I need to get to bed because I have school tomorrow. Bye, Diary!

♡ The Owl Times ♡

Friday

School was so much fun tonight, Diary! Mrs. Featherbottom told us about a new project we'll be working on this week.

> We are going to create a class newspaper called the Owl Times! Everyone will have a special job.

We each chose a job . . .

Carlos:
cartoonist

Zac:
weather reporter

Macy:
editor

Lilly:
sports reporter

Sue:
fashion writer

Zara:
photographer

Jacob:
travel writer

George:
designer

Lucy:
crossword puzzle
writer

I chose <u>news reporter</u>. It was the perfect job for me! I love asking questions. And I love writing.

Everyone was excited about their jobs — especially Zara! She started taking photos right away!

The first piece of news I heard was from Mrs. Featherbottom:

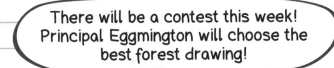

There will be a contest this week! Principal Eggmington will choose the best forest drawing!

The winning drawing will be published in our newspaper. And the winner will win two movie tickets to <u>Wingderella</u>!

Wow! I hope I win, Diary! I'd give my extra ticket to Lucy so we could see **WINGDERELLA** together!!

At recess, I talked to my classmates and kept my ears open for more news. Here's what I found out:

George has a new hat.

Kiera and her family are on vacation in **HOOTALULU**.

Sue's mom is designing a dress for famous actress Fifi Flyaway.

Macy's pet frog, Wilber, won "Best in Show" last weekend.

This news was all exciting. But I heard the <u>best</u> news after recess . . .

This was **FLAP-TASTIC** news!
Everyone spent the rest of the day
talking about the new owl.

Lucy and I were both excited to meet Hailey.

Now I must get to bed. Good day!

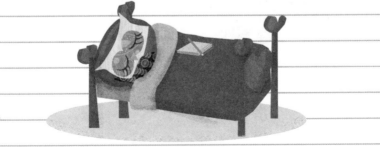

♡ Meany McMeanerson! ♡

Saturday

I love being busy, Diary. This is a good thing – because I ended up being crazy busy tonight!

I wrote a to-do list of everything I wanted to get done this weekend. (I even added a couple of things to help make Hailey feel super welcome on her first day at school!)

1. Get my feathers cut (It is about time!)

2. Draw the best forest drawing

3. Keep reporting for the class newspaper (I'll write down any news I hear!)

4. Make Hailey a necklace

5. Make Hailey a guide to Treetopolis

First, I went to the **FEATHERDRESSER**. But I wasn't the only owl there . . .

Sue Clawson was there! She is always getting her feathers done. And her claws. And her eyelashes. And her wing tips.

Now, Diary, sometimes Sue can be nice. And sometimes Sue can be mean.

Nice Sue

Mean Sue

Sometimes I call her Meany McMeanerson.

Then I flew home to work on my drawing. Lucy stopped by.

It took me a LONG time to finish my drawing. But it looks good! I'm just not sure if it's good enough to win. What do you think, Diary?

My to-do list isn't even half finished, but the sun is coming up. It looks like tomorrow is going to be another crazy-busy night! I must get to sleep!

4

♡ Busy, Busy, Busy ♡

Sunday

Tonight started off with some reporting for the newspaper...

I heard Mom on the phone with Lilly's mom.

Lilly's mom had just talked to George's mom.

George's little sister Jenny had sprained her wing playing **WINGBALL**.

Poor Jenny!

I called Zara and asked her to meet me at George's house. I interviewed Jenny while Zara took photos.

When I got home, I still had two things left on my to-do list:

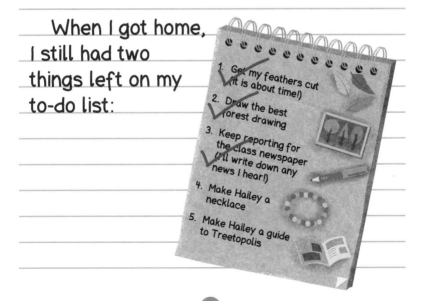

I got right to work!

First, I made a **FLAPERRIFIC** bead necklace.

Here it is:

Then Lucy called.

Eva, guess what! I have a new puppet-show theater!

Wow! That's wing-tastic!

Do you want to come over to play with it?

Sorry, but I'm busy making things for Hailey's first day.

That's nice of you! Well, I guess I'll see you at school tomorrow.

Yes! Bye, Lucy!

Finally, I finished the guide.
Check it out!

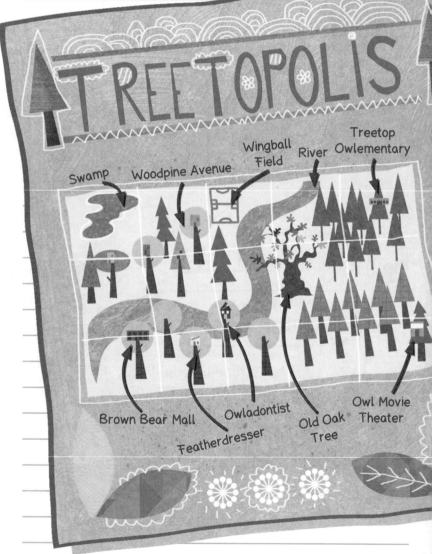

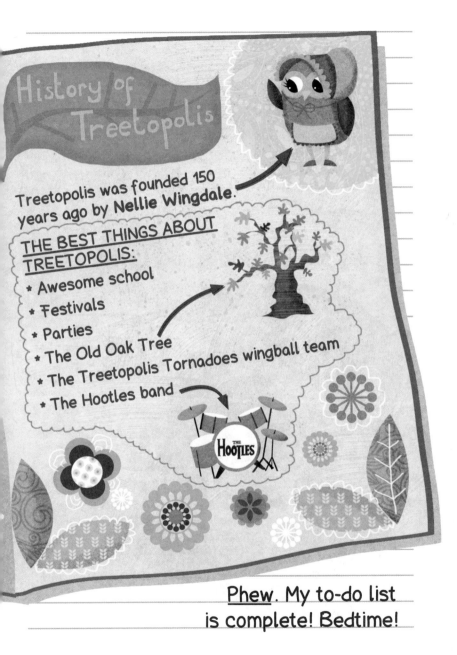

History of Treetopolis

Treetopolis was founded 150 years ago by **Nellie Wingdale**.

<u>THE BEST THINGS ABOUT TREETOPOLIS:</u>

* Awesome school
* Festivals
* Parties
* The Old Oak Tree
* The Treetopolis Tornadoes wingball team
* The Hootles band

<u>Phew</u>. My to-do list is complete! Bedtime!

♡ The New Owl ♡

Monday

Lucy and I flew to school together.

Eva, my new puppet-show theater is so cool!

I can't wait to see it!

32

33

Lucy and I normally sit next to each other in class. But, Diary, I was just SO excited to meet the new owl!

I'm worried that Lucy felt a bit sad about me changing seats. But I didn't want Hailey to have to sit next to Meany McMeanerson on her first day.

Then Hailey flew into the classroom!

Class, I'd like you all to meet Hailey.

Hello.

Hailey, please sit wherever you'd like.

I waved my wings in the air and pointed at the empty seat next to me.

But I guess Hailey didn't see me because she sat next to Lucy instead. In my old seat.

We all turned in our forest drawings. Then Mrs. Featherbottom said Hailey could work on the crossword puzzle with Lucy.

I sat on my own and wrote my story about George's sister.

I planned to give Hailey the necklace and the guide after school. But things didn't go as planned.

I flew up to Hailey after school.

I couldn't tell if Hailey <u>really</u> liked the necklace. She took it. But I felt silly as I flew away.

I decided not to give Hailey the guide until tomorrow. I want to look it over again, to make sure it looks <u>really</u> good. I hope she'll like it more than she liked the necklace. Sleep well, Diary.

♥ It's All Going Wrong! ♥

Tuesday

Hi Diary,

Lucy and I flew to school together. But we didn't say much. Do you think Lucy feels bad that Hailey sat next to her and not me?

School wasn't much better tonight. We worked on the newspaper, which was great. But Hailey sat next to Lucy again. The two of them were laughing like the best of friends.

I also saw Hailey talking with Sue.

I felt a bit sad. I still hoped that Hailey would want to be my friend, too. And I hoped my guide would make everything better.

I finally gave the guide to Hailey after school.

Hi, Hailey! I made this for you. It shows a map of Treetopolis. There's a list of places to visit and everything.

Wow, Eva! That's so sweet of you! But I already sort of know my way around. Sue gave me a tour.

Oh.

Your guide is pretty, though! I'd love to hang it up at home, if that's okay.

Oh, Diary! I just felt so silly! My cheeks went red.

I flew home as quickly as I could.

Mom knew I was upset. Moms always do. She gave me a warm cup of **BUG CHOCOLATE**, a hug, and some good advice.

You can't <u>make</u> friendships happen, Eva. You should always be yourself and hope that others like you for who you are.

I know, Mom. I just <u>really</u> want Hailey to like me.

Diary, I feel MUCH better. My plan for tomorrow: invite Hailey to sleep over!

♡ Sleepover Disaster! ♡

We all had fun working on the <u>Owl Times</u> in school tonight.

I finished writing the news story about George's sister Jenny.

Lucy and Hailey finished working on
their crossword puzzle.

Zara kept
taking pictures of
EVERYONE all
the time.

Zac reported
the weather to us
(whether we wanted
to know it or not)!

Carlos drew funny cartoons of each of us.

Lilly wrote about our **WINGBALL** game for the sports page.

Jacob wrote about **OWLANDO** for the travel page. (His family went on vacation there.) And Sue wrote about what owls <u>should</u> and <u>should not</u> wear.

George designed the front page. And Macy checked everything for mistakes.

It was exciting to see our newspaper coming together!

After school, I flew up to Hailey.

Hi, Hailey!

Hi, Eva!

I wanted to see if, um, you maybe wanted to come over for a sleepover on Saturday.

That's really thoughtful of you, Eva! Thank you! But, well, I'm sorry — I've already agreed to sleep over at Lucy's this Saturday. Maybe you could ask Lucy if you can come, too?

I flew off before Hailey finished talking. I felt embarrassed. Again.

When I got home, I tried to cheer myself up. I dressed Baxter in a pink ballerina outfit. But then my brother, Humphrey, came into my room . . .

Who's ever heard of a "bat-erina"? Baxter looks so silly!

Oh, you're such a squirrel-head, Humphrey!

I wasn't having <u>any</u> fun without Lucy. So I called her.

Hi, Lucy.

Hi, Eva.

Just wondered what you were doing?

I'm busy, Eva.

Oh.

Well you've been busy this week, too.

Oh. I guess so.

Bye, Eva.

Diary, I think I may have lost my very best <u>old</u> friend by trying SO hard to make a <u>new</u> friend. Maybe Sue was right. Why would Hailey want to be friends with me? She only wants to be friends with cool owls, and Lucy is <u>the coolest</u>.

8

♡ And the Winner Is . . . ♡

Thursday

I flew to school all by myself tonight.

Principal Eggmington flew into our class. He came to tell us who had won the forest drawing contest.

All of your artwork was flaperrific! But I chose the most colorful drawing and the one that looked like it had taken the longest to make. The winner is . . .

I held my breath.

I won! I couldn't believe it! Everyone clapped as I flew up to collect my prize.

Now I have two tickets to see **WINGDERELLA** on Saturday!

But Diary, I don't have a best friend to take with me anymore. It really looks like Hailey is Lucy's new best friend.

After school, all I wanted to do was hang out with Lucy. But I've really messed that up. So I made some new puppets instead.

Here's me and Lucy:

I even made little Baxter and Rex puppets.

I pretended I was playing with them in Lucy's new puppet-show theater. Puppet Eva and Puppet Lucy are best friends. I just wish the <u>real</u> Eva and Lucy were, too.

Humphrey saw me playing with the puppets. I thought he was going to make fun of me. But he didn't . . .

Eva, you have been moping around for ages. I'm bored of it. Why don't you just say sorry to Lucy?

Because I'm worried Lucy doesn't want to be my friend anymore. You see, I haven't been very nice to her this week. I didn't hang out with her. And I didn't sit next to her. Really, all I've talked about this week is the new owl.

Humphrey is right. (Not about my extra movie ticket!) I know what I need to do. Don't worry, Diary. I have a BIG plan to fix everything!

♥ A BIG Sorry ♥

Friday

I flew to school super early tonight, Diary. Mrs. Featherbottom was the only owl there.

I placed a newspaper on each desk.

Everyone started reading as soon as they got to class!

The Owl Times

Owl Always Love You

BY EVA WINGDALE

I learned something big this week: friendship is tricky. When I tried to make a new friend, I nearly lost an old friend. My oldest, _bestest_ friend — Lucy Beakman. Lucy always makes me happy, always has time for me, and always lends a helping wing when I need one. I know now that while it's great to make new friends, we must never forget how special our old friendships are. (Lucy, I'm so sorry. I miss you.)

Me and Lucy when we were baby owlets

Lucy looked up after she read the article. I flew over.

I handed Lucy my movie tickets.

You and Hailey should go see
<u>Wingderella</u> before your sleepover.

Thank you, Eva! But I want you to come
to the sleepover, too! Besides, your
drawing was amazing! I couldn't see
<u>Wingderella</u> without you.

Hailey must have heard us talking.
She flew right over.

What if the three of us chipped in to pay
for a third ticket? Then we could all go!

That's a great idea!

That would be owlsome!

Just then, I realized another BIG thing about friendship: the more, the merrier!

Who else wants to come to the movies tomorrow?

Everyone raised their wings! Then Mrs. Featherbottom **HOOTED**:

Eva has perfect timing, class! Principal Eggmington said he was so impressed with your newspaper that we can <u>all</u> take a field trip to the movies!

Now everyone can go!

♡ Sleepover Success! ♡

Saturday

I flew over to Lucy's house as soon as I woke up tonight. I showed her the puppets I made.

I love them!

We put on a puppet show for Baxter and Rex! It was such a **HOOT**!

Then Hailey came over. The three of us chose outfits for the field trip. We all looked **FLAP-TASTIC**!!! Hailey even wore the necklace I gave her!

Here's a photo of ALL of us at the movies tonight. (Kiera came back from vacation just in time!)

Now I've got to run, Diary, or I'll be late for the sleepover with my newest and oldest best friends — Hailey and Lucy! See you next week!

Rebecca Elliott was a lot like Eva when she was younger: She loved making things and hanging out with her best friends. Now that Rebecca is older, not much has changed — except that her best friends are her husband, Matthew, and their children. She still loves making things, like stories, cakes, music, and paintings. But as much as she and Eva have in common, Rebecca cannot fly or turn her head all the way around. No matter how hard she tries.

Rebecca is the author of JUST BECAUSE and MR. SUPER POOPY PANTS. OWL DIARIES is her first early chapter book series.

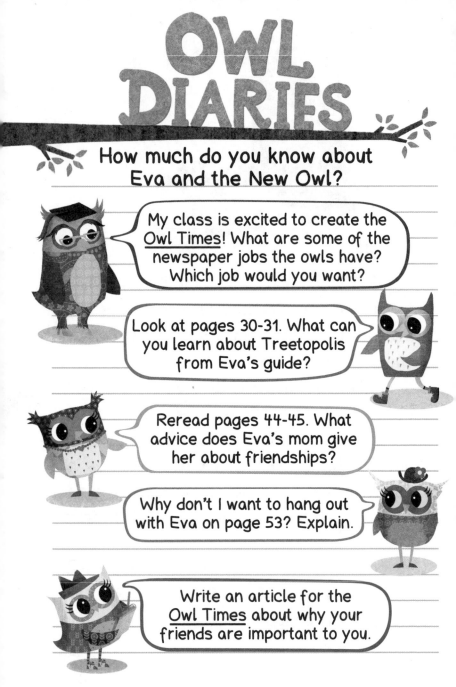

OWL DIARIES

How much do you know about Eva and the New Owl?

My class is excited to create the <u>Owl Times</u>! What are some of the newspaper jobs the owls have? Which job would you want?

Look at pages 30-31. What can you learn about Treetopolis from Eva's guide?

Reread pages 44-45. What advice does Eva's mom give her about friendships?

Why don't I want to hang out with Eva on page 53? Explain.

Write an article for the <u>Owl Times</u> about why your friends are important to you.

2/28 Mary Cate Sr 2

St. Agnes School